CU00705188

Glean & Graft

Fresher
The Publishing House for New Voices

Bournemouth
University

Glean & Graft

A Bournemouth Writing Prize anthology

First published 2021 by Fresher Publishing

Fresher Publishing
Bournemouth University
Weymouth House
Fern Barrow
Poole
Dorset BH12 5BB

www.fresherpublishing.co.uk

Email: escattergood@bournemouth.ac.uk

Editors: Laila Lock, Modupe Olajumoke Alaga,
Manuela Vițelaru and Holly Miles

Artwork by: Ginny Phillips

Acknowledgements

We would like to extend our thanks to the talented poets from around the world who made this anthology possible. Our particular gratitude goes to Bournemouth Writing Prize judges, poets Antony Dunn and Tom Masters. We also greatly appreciate the input of cover designer, Ginny Phillips, who captured the essence of our concept.

Contents

Sow: beginnings

Foreword

This collection of poems, selected from entries to The Bournemouth Writing Prize during the lockdown of 2020/21, is a true celebration of the human experience in these uncertain times.

Just as many of us have found solace in nature, this anthology looks to the rhythms of the land for its structure, while also offering something for all moods and moments.

Dip inside these pages and you will find both the bizarre and the normative sitting comfortably together providing an honest appraisal of life, love and loss.

It was our privilege to glean these unique poems for you and hope they provide you with a rewarding and enjoyable reading experience.

With best wishes,

Manuela Vitelaru, Modupe Olajumoke Alaga, Holly Miles and Laila Lock (Editors)

The Bournemouth Writing Prize is run annually by Fresher Publishing at Bournemouth University, and this anthology was created by students of BU's MA Creative Writing & Publishing.
www.fresherpublishing.co.uk

Blight

My Father's Hands

by Alison Nuorto

My father was always ashamed of his hands.
Of those misshapen digits:
The result of a childhood accident.
Juvenile jibes made him self-conscious:
He dreaded handshakes and parties.
Nicotine smudges and brittle, bitten down nails,
Heightened their unloveliness.
In old age, his ill-fitting Wedding band, had to be
wedged on.
Those hands had endured too many winters.
His hands never could fill adult gloves.
Limply, the fingers would droop, resembling chickens.
As a child, I would trace the outline of his hands,
And run a finger along jagged nails, embedded in
meaty flesh.
As I got older, I resented how much my hands
resembled his.
Not quite a pianist's hands: octaves were a struggle.
Occasional remarks gave birth to my inheritance of
shame.
But, as he lay on the sterilized sheet,
And the shrill beeping jabbed at my grief,
In filial observance, I placed my hands over his.
In wordless, inexhaustible grief.

2 a.m.

by Jess Fallon-Ford

I've seen a lot of things during lockdown.
'Lockdown'.
Funny how the meaning of a word can evolve into something else. Metamorphosed by certain contexts and conditions. It might well have meant something different back then. In relation to war maybe. Or terror.' We are now commencing lockdown' might be heard over the crackle of a speakerphone. Cries of 'school shooter' can be heard ricocheting off the walls in the background. But this is a different kind of war. What was I saying again?
The world seems so complex it resembles that of a cotton ball. Only the threads are so criss-crossed and twisted into knots that really it doesn't resemble this at all. The colour is seeping out. Spilling.
Gushing. Into a union of grey.
The sound of wind and steel cuts through the night. Not a plane. That's a rare sight nowadays. A few days is all it takes to change everything and so far it's taken five to find him. They say the first seventy-two hours are crucial in a missing persons' case. Here it comes again, chopping up the night into a noisy haze. Some might even call it a nuisance.
How quintessential.

2 a.m.

He probably felt the same way. A nuisance to his own life.
I note the sky has adopted a deep shade of purple-black, almost like a bruise.

Brave

by Georgia Cowley

Once there was a little girl,
Who'd never whinge or pine.
She always had a smile for you,
Her name was Caroline.

When all the other little girls,
Blubbed and brayed and bawled,
They said, "Why can't you be like her?"
Then turn away, appalled.

And when she fell and scraped her knee
They'd rush on her with praise:
"Our Caroline would never cry."
"Our Caroline's so brave."

Until one day small, wirey threads
Of sadness, hurt and doubt,
Sprouted deep in Caroline,
And found no pathway out.

They tangled up inside of her,
They'd twist her, pinch and pull.
They grew and grew all over her,
Till Caroline was full.

Soon the tangled spider's web,
Formed a knotty noose,
And Caroline began to fear,
She'd never pry them loose.

Still our girl did not cry out,
Even as she died,
Keeping in the messy thoughts
We've all been taught to hide.

"How terrible" They all bemoaned
Standing at her grave.
"If only she had asked our help."
"If she only she'd been brave."

'poetry, n.'
by C T Mills

/ 'po ʊ ɪ tri /
1 literary work in verse

2 solace   in line breaks, i curl
       up-   in you, i take comfort in the whip and
way of
         rhyme and

3 inspiration
i am denise riley's lover. that is to say, i know her
intimately, which here means too well
we grieve the same, in rags, scrabbling in the dirt for a
glimpse of your soul
were you ever even here?

4 grief is hungry and i feed him sad songs because
my hands are shaking

too hard to cook a real dinner, because night has
fallen, and you are still
not home

5 i-

Stop the Train

by Helen Ribchester

Please stop the train, I want to get off.
You see, I never was meant to get on.
I've had no time to think or plan
now the life I expected has gone.

I accept it's my lot, my fate and my turn
To fight with this dreaded disease.
But I wasn't ready, I wasn't prepared,
So, for a minute, just stop the train please.

I need time to cry,
Time to rant and to rave.
Time to contempl...

Triptychs at Safe Haven Dementia Home

by Jane Thomas

Next door is Mavis, likes the colour yellow and Miles
Davis, used to be a nurse.
The other side is Percy, he was in the army, fought in
France, likes baked beans.
Across the way is Mary, likes teddy bears, throwing
punches and purple peonies.

[Upstairs are the old timers, but don't worry about the
screams, they stop at six.]

In the kitchen is Harry, likes Special Brew, B&H and
being on parole.
Cleaning the loo is Tia, speaks Tagalog, vegan, misses
her daughters.
Front of house is Chloe, likes New Look,
amphetamines and Bumble.

Fill in three facts about your father and we will put it
in the book
and in an aluminium frame on his door.

Welcome...

White Water, Leather Too

by Whitney Glover

You freeze at the sound, sure that you're caught.
A moment of respite, finally, from the high tide of
your hand in my throat.
Teaching politeness like the role model you are, I can
choke easier now.
It feels like realising I've been drowned, when I'm at
the bottom of the ocean
Because I've been choking since then.
Why wouldn't you breathe? you're asking, and I hear
it like an unwanted heartbeat in my chest.
Why aren't you okay? you're shouting, and I hear it
like an unwanted heartbeat between my legs.
Keep it all quiet. I'm hearing, and you beg with hands
that like to touch what isn't theirs for mercy that will
always be yours.
Naïve as I am, I hoped to share air, but there is no
sharing here,
And the thought of borrowing stings like sea salt in
the wound of a favour.
You'd lend me my life back? Dust it off and shove it
back inside me? Leave it stupid slick so it comes out
smooth on the slide?
If I could find my spine, I'd hand it to you to beat me
with
And make me stop chewing on nerves.
The ebb and flow of this ache will always have its

moon, it was designed to be held, not to hold, and the
three states of matter haven't heard about you.
I freeze at the sound, sure that I'm caught.
The sediment of rot in me moves, shivering, I'm back
at the surface, gasping, watching for danger as it
keeps me afloat.
You know this before I tell you, how it's lingering
under us like the smell of rain.
There are breaths I will never take.
There are waves that will never crash.

Hello, My Strength

by Beth Steiner

Your face, shiny and apple-tipped,
turned towards me in your natural disco lights.
Your eyes, ink stained but painted gold,
watch my hands, desperately idle,
but not always my feet
as they trip the light-mediocre
on my handmade tightrope.
You hold my hands to stop me scratching,
but you never cut my nails.

And I can see your reflection
in the peppered tea we drink from one cup.
You were there to pick up the pieces on the beach.
As I wouldn't, couldn't, didn't, still can't
go on.
And as you beat with the scent of warmth and willing,
we huddle in the road while I shiver
like a rusty rabbit, wide-eyed and full of holes.

A Peculiar Dream

by Stewart Arnold

Such a peculiar dream
it lingered yet raced by somehow
Sitting with old schoolfriends
their names elude me now

But why was I chased
by the man with an angry face?
I tried my very best to run
my feet rooted in one place

I remember falling
from a cliff edge, down an endless dark shaft
with such a thud I landed
Who was it who laughed?

Could it have been the clown
or the beggar at my knees
as we floated 'cross a river
on a raft of purple trees

Three fierce dogs faced me
as I knelt weeping in the rain
Someone said 'there, there'
and tied me with a chain

A Peculiar Dream

In a flash, the dream was a shadow
Precious relief was mine to keep,
shaking, 'twas then I realised
I had not been asleep

A Sociological Sigh

by Beth Steiner

The rain on the cherries is their colour:
Crimson, magenta, Nazi blood.
Freshness is our generation's opiate,
pain our consolation.
We display our soulless assertion
over our infancy,
and take more pills to dull the ache
in our one head -
The guilt of our bloody atheism.
And all the while we lust
for the youthful bends of Oblivion,
searching for the crooked cures
of our childhood.
And a bigger bowl of cherries.

Calming
by Victoria Helen Loftus

The road ahead
thick with smog

An outstretched hand
vanishes as it tries to grab onto
Something
Anything to comfort the
juttering jitterbug of jagged
Something

Can't eat
Can't sleep
Can't speak

No analogy to make you understand
To twist this fraying ribbon into a neat little loop
And help you to navigate the swamplands to
the cinderblock citadel constructed to protect the
thoughts -
That escape like snakes and bite me

Bite you
Bite anyone

I try to see the light shining through the tunnel,
But it's just a mirage
A decoy to catch the roadrunner
I pull a muscle just to feel something
Breathing in time with the

CLA-CLUNK
CLA-CLUNK
CLA-CLUNK

Of a washing machine spin cycle

Inhale-exhale

Threatening

To penetrate this artificial calm

Cat's Got My Tongue
by Penny Dedman

I want to speak of her and how hope can survive as
the shattered world dismantles our dreams and
she, like me, is locked in a stillness of waiting. She
smiled like a slight when we first met and circled each
other with the sniffing suspicion of new animals; her
mouth Minnelli-red; me with Heidi plaits. We were
a joyous chiaroscuro, our lips pursed for wine and
tirades, but each mindful to give berth to our
differences. Now hope is waving a white flag. I see
her fade with the sickness sinking its fangs into
her flesh, and breathless, we watch the past curving
and crashing towards today. We will it to swerve or
stop, either will do. Years ago her man asked me
to stay by her side in the weeks before he died,
gifting me his discourse of hope:
 "She's your best friend you know, as you are for her."
Fear is the wall, the distance between us, recumbent,
lolling in lockdown.
I can't speak
my heart.
Cat's got my tongue.

Fault of Innocence

by Pixie Davies

Darkness fades to light, I wake.
Tapping at my door, a friendly smile.
Safety enters the room.
A hug, whispered words, promises.
A hand, a simple hand, travels to places unknown.
Fear creeps in. This isn't safety.
This is evil.

I cry for him to stop.
I beg, I plead.
I am scared.
He rewards me.
Money in the pot.
I'm his plaything.

I get brave.
I fight.
He stops, he blames, he accuses.
I know nothing.
He leaves.
He is the wolf in sheep's clothing.

I am the lamb.
Slaughtered and defiled.
My innocence lost.
My fault.
I am alone.
I am 12...

I am a child,
He is my abuser...
A trusted adult no more.
I am alone.
The monster haunts my dreams.
The beast waits in the darkness.
I am alone.

I am 34...
Scars won't heal.
Haunted and broken.
The beast still lurking.
In my head, always.

The pain.
The memory.
The horror.

Fallow

Leaf Storm

by Dara Kavanagh

i.m. my mother

Some days after the diagnosis
set time, a death-watch beetle,
ticking, you set out undaunted
for the park. Your time of year -
air cold as water, the trees
touched with fleeting majesty.
As we rounded a beech copse,
a puckish wind stirred up and,
like Dante's fugitives, drove all
about a streaming leaf storm,
shoal-dense and endless, brass
after brass, chattering, sheering
in great murmurations, showing
the raw grandeur in letting go.

The May Zephyr

by Aoife Khan

As the morning sun glares
They know we are gifted prevaricators
The self-anointed crown which we wore
Has been surrendered with dutiful grace

Still, I do not quail
In this defeat there is no tender aching
Herculean in its standing, was our false reign
Our exile is not fruitless

The tired soil of this earth
Now beckons our bodies too
In honest arms
Let us hold each other once more

Here, where the late spring gale has dispersed the
poppy seeds
We shall rest
Come summer, come the May zephyr
The red petals will fall gently over our blighted bones
Perhaps in time, the ferryman can look at us again

Lost Intimacy

by Eleanor Jones

Only when the liquor licks at my lips do I contemplate
calling your number
Having no real hope that you might answer, letting it
ring out into the night
Imagining still to whisper your name and recall the
times you called out mine.
To confess of my continued longing and the want that
is yet to waiver.
What a terror it truly turned out to be, to crave a
sweet scoundrel so.

I have been learning to breathe again since your lips
parted mine
For you left me dumbfounded and desperately dazed,
Stupefied by such splendour, by the sweetness of your
kiss.
Won't you lay me down again lover and snatch my
breath once more?

I was bound not broken when I found bliss beneath
your body weight
Hands tied and hopes high, your mouth explored the
rest of me
Arched backs and mouths agape, your tongue was
poetry in motion.

Leaving me squirming in sensual delight, desperate
for more of you.
You would plant kisses across my skin and watch
them bloom.
Spring wildflowers would adorn my every curve and
crease,
Trails of delicate memories where your mouth freely
explored every inch of me;
A meadow of gentle worship, of love and lust
combined

I remain haunted by the memory of my head upon
your chest,
The warmth your skin radiated under sheets that
smelled of us,
Your candlelight glow and the shapes your shadows
made.
Both the dream and the nightmare, these little lost
intimacies

My Body is a Canvas

by Jess Fallon-Ford

My body is a canvas marked by Time
herself.
Don't get me wrong- I am no picture
perfect painting.
I am impressionist.
See the scars that
> dance
>> upon
>>> my
>>>> skin?

The scars society says shouldn't be
allowed?
They complete my masterpiece.

The Chaining of the Dead

by Manuela Vițelaru

August was cruelly hot, troubling my thoughts, burned
corn lanes down into long lines of ashes, scattered
our hopes and fears into white dust, triggered
traumatic memories of loss and misfortune from
March.

I heard many exchanged poems on Instagram
and holiday memories of sunsets from previous years.
Talking of which, I remember watching the sun setting
down in your hazel green eyes. O how sweet!

If freedom were a person, her life would be taken too
soon...
Poor Freedom! She'll be deeply missed and mourned!

There're no windows to the outside world, no... escape
or light, only an opaque wooden framed canvas,
an unpainted one, on which I'd love to one day blend
some red and yellow acrylics to re-create
a sunset—for this falling world— and a sweet memory too,
of light shining behind grey clouds, silver fog
and traffic smoke— I miss seeing you in person terribly,
by the way, and it's as if I could see you and I here and
now
together again, holding the brush, although physically
apart,

yet sharing this moment of white silence—
Hold it still, please, until I come see you for real,
hopefully, still sane by then...

At night, I usually dream of golden corn lanes—
light piercing through the broken reeds,
music symphonies exalted to the sky! Then silence
creeps, going off louder and louder in my mind—I'm
alone

and I awake in panic, losing my breath— where's your
hand?
Frightened, I lift my hands up from under
my damp bedsheet, towards the sky, feeling as though
the ceiling's lowering down to crush me between
two palms. My hope's much stronger than my mind!
And will I live enough to see this time change?

Perhaps I'd become a fading daffodil pressed between
a book's pages, telling a bedtime story about dandling
time
itself on my knees— but wait, there was no spring,
no summer this year, no sun and shadows on the
streets,
no people, or rain or songs— people were numb—
and no caressing hand for the yellow daffodils.

So, I watched the mould flowers growing rapidly
on my cold bedroom wall, spreading green and black,
and in dark algae hues of cracked layers of paint.
So dull! And I felt lonely, yet content.

Harrow

Time to Go Home

by Nancy Ward

On the edge,
I take a spoon
of what once was you
then scatter ash
into the air and
hold my breath
as, with your usual flair,
bones
turn into fairy dust
and you dance your last dance
with a diamond smile,
a comet's tail
dropping for one more
skinny dip.
And there you drift,
Suspended
still sparkling,
still reluctant
to disperse,
to admit the party's over.
And so am I.

Intuition

by Ruth Wells

Trusting my intuition
Is counter intuitive
I've been socially conditioned
To trust that it's transgressive.
To dissent to my intuit,
Deemed emotive, and I knew it
Wouldn't wash.

So, I try to stick to the linear
To the cerebral, to the rational.
Have a rationale for decisions
That would pass a deep analysis.
A paralysis of feelings
Means I'm taken semi-serious.
But appearances are deceptive
And it's crept in despite this,

My irrepressible intuition

If I listen,
If I listen,
Maybe if I listen,
It can steer me,
If I hear me.
If I trust the voice I've silenced,
It can guide me,

And you'll find me
In my innermost interior,
Not inferior
Not inferior
But mother-fucking superior.

My unsurpassable intuition

I'm going to thread them together
My intuit and my brain
Weave them with dream threads
And all the hope I can find.
No longer at war, they will hold a shalom
For I long to be whole
With my heart and my mind.

The Other Woman
by Elizabeth M Castillo

The sun has set, and at this hour,
shadows hang between the daylight and the trees.
There, the sudden scent of blood,
      scent of man,
carries to me on the breeze, the wind
howling through, falls silent at my feet:
      "Good hunting, milady,"
it whispers, then retreats. There is
a darkness in this forest, an end
that rivals death itself,
in the mist about my ankles. Even lizards
know they would do well to hide
inside their hovels, and underground.

Dirt crunches beneath.
      Treacherous soil!
Leaves plunge downwards,
to be eaten by the earth.
The naked trees testify, this forest is deadly,
and will swallow you whole. I hear
footsteps racing, running, in thundering lockstep.
Flash of black. Flash of teeth.
      There are dangerous games afoot!
Surely it's time to turn back. Surely it's time to go home.
I am well beyond my borders now.
She can't catch me, she can't catch me,

here, where I lurk and linger on the periphery,
just out of sight, just beyond her mind's eye.
She knows I am here, her veins
course with rage, and vengeance.
But she does not know where.
She is death. She is danger.
But the line has been crossed,
the threat prowls within her marked territory.
She may think I have lost,
but this no longer bears any resemblance to a fair
fight. No, now two legs, not enough.
I drop down onto four,
draw strength from the thousand invisible
hertbeats, the lifeblood,
the microbiome of the forest floor.

There is fear, and some fury,
encrusted under each hungry claw. The hunts
smells of my father, champion long before I
had ever heard of this sport, and I wonder:
would he be proud?
There is sweat at my temples, and my wrists are bound
to stop them from trembling.
I step, crabways, low and feral, without shadow
or sound. Your ears twitch and you shudder,
neck craning to see what you
and I must learn the hard way;
the deadliest thing in here is me.

There Was Never Any Poetry, Just Blood

by Elizabeth M Castillo

There was no poetry that day; just blood.
My memory now-
a haze, a jumble of that day,
some far-removed anecdote I heard.
from a girl I met on the plane
one day, (I think she had my eyes),
but she was smaller than me. Better skin,
and still believed all these things,
all this mess,
amounted to some sort of poetry.

There was no one home that day,
just me, and what remained of her.
And perhaps... no. The children? I'm not sure.
There was the staircase, with no banister.
Terrible architectural flaw. Two legs,
visible, from the calves down,
and the crying- always the crying.
That morbid, melancholic sound.
"What now?" went the thoughts, "What's happened
today?"
I cleared the corner, eyes riveted
on the top of the stairs, where she stood wailing,
waving frantically, wrists bared. I'm not sure
I understood. I'm not sure
I knew how to care.

There's no memory of what happened,
just the noise, and the blood.
And the guilt, as I looked in her eyes-my eyes,
as we sat in 31C and D. I should really
have felt something. So much blood, her blood,
the very stuff that makes us. But I've found,
there's only so much a young mind can take in
at any one time. I should
have felt something, done something. Been
something.
Been enough. Even now, as I try to stitch the memory
back together, I am convinced:
there was never any poetry. There was only ever
blood.

Weathered Sketches

by Jess Fallon-Ford

See how the colours dance in the sky?
We're all like that.
Pigments of colour crossing paths
on one iridescent canvas.
A myriad of masterpieces,
each one different from the next.
Some are coloured in yellows and pinks
and finished with a soft golden hue.
The very beginnings of a sunset.
Others are void of any colour at all,
shrouded in black and faded
grey at the edges.
Weathered sketches left out in the rain
waiting to be painted yellow again.

Voices on a Bus

by Yvette Appleby

I take my seat ready for the play to begin

Make way for the track suited ladies / bare midriffs /
designer pushchairs / screaming babies
Ignored / Intent on their phone / they text / they call /
they bawl
one sided explosion of sounds/ the shouting / the
swearing / the put downs
They are done / tell the unseen to do one
The lull / the cooling off / contact once more
To start the war again / to have the final word / it's
absurd

Things that go on in her head / words unsaid / silently
replying to a screen
Where you at he says / oh my days like I can go
anywhere / the look / the accusation stare
He hates that I go out with my mates / berates / creates
a scene
Why am I with him?
Incoming!... Word bombs
What you seen / what you read
What you mean / what you said
Replying through her fingertips
Ignores her words / silent scream / don't forget my
kebab and chips

Schoolboy in front / books / looks / anxious eyes / head
is full
Brain is racing / pacing / repeating / speaking to no-
one but himself
I try to learn but really want to burn every page
Numbers / /equations / additions / divisions / I cannot
reason with this
Disentangle all these facts from the humming mass
behind my eyes
The whys/ wherefores / lost and done for / all ambition
dies
If I don't pass will I spontaneously combust?

Driver looks up / you on the top deck / I see you
The wheels on the bus go round and round / the noise
on the bus goes pound and pound
All day long / how long / three more hours
Tickets out of date mate / waiting for the foul berate /
leave the bus or pay
Not your day / no way / Gets off / hits the mirror kicks
the door
Driver sighs and moves on / others look at the floor

Elbow in my eye / backside in my face/ someone
getting on someone's case
I just want to chill with no fuss but that will never
happen on the 97 bus
Getting off / reaching home / some peace within reach
Eat sleep repeat

Bogotá

by Lyz Pfister

So this is where the water took us:
your country
dry like a highway, dusty
old men with Aguilas and Achiras
in plastic packs
and every window slashed with bars
whether the treasures are golden
bottles of whisky or wrinkle-skinned empanadas.

Here, the only familiar thing
is your hand on my leg
and your incomprehensible Spanish,
here is where it's like to live
inside your own mind
is to live inside the ship's harbour
and under the boat, choked
on salt.

But here, there is no sea
and no boat, only
splintered asphalt, brownish
and broad-leafed bushes, buses
spilling smoke,
broken red bricks and burned-
looking dogs.
I'm a stranger here, but I promised

Bogota

this place my heart, hard
as it is to give
my mouth to a language I don't speak,
my tongue to a food I can't taste,
my eyes to rust-coloured wind,
my ears to an aching accordion,
my mind to myself

and you, when you remember
other homes, how we built
one in a place that was neither yours
nor mine,
how we both belong
to more than each other,
how one of us will always wander,
if we both don't.

Night Watch

by Manuela Vițelaru

Speak your life to this desolate rondure
Weave your waves with dry seaweed, and rest
Your heart on mine; like slithering, dusted
Sand lines, blow mysteries now forgotten.

Behold, the starless sky resembles
A heavy, sombre heart that rests against
Horizon's end. A salt-tensed air is sensed
As freezing breeze like breath awakens

Some seagulls, one metre apart, commence
A wailing song; wide open eyes confess
With beacon light towards a troubled sea:

An alley of death masked by bright pretence,
Slumberously drowning into regress...
'Til daylight finds us, and we shall see.

Missed Chances

by Charlotte Rudman

This year
showed us how
the current of time
cannot be measured or mastered
no instrument or tool
can grapple with
or put into numbers
or put into words
or find a way
to mark the rising tide
days and days and
days, with no separation
between what was and what will be:
what is today?
when is tomorrow?
was there a last week?
Missed chances
huddled with school friends
and plus-ones
sharing a hipflask
of something strong
that no one really likes
while one ties the knot.
No open house at new flats
the next day covering
wine stains

not cramming the table
made for 6 with 10
making a roast that won't be ready
for another 3 hours...
no drop-ins for tea
no "I'm in the area"
no "oh go on then"
finishing the bottle
laughing with the
expectation of hangovers
a stolen hug
a-quick-squeeze
a kiss on the head
brief moments of touch
now all lost
to the currents
in a year that time forgot.

Dancing with Ghosts

by Kødiak

There's a ghost who lives between these walls
and he's me, or at least he responds to my name.
His hand passes through mine and we stumble and fall,
while we dance amongst all of our fears and shame.

The wiring in this apartment isn't "quirky",
like you always used to say; it's faulty.
Broken light switches and cracked memories
(from before you left) of who we used to be.

I still remember when we would hit the bars.
A slowly melting cube of ice circling the glass
of bourbon from a bottle I could hardly afford, or
pizza by the slice to a soundtrack of drifting jazz.

In a city filled with ghosts and Spanish moss,
I guess I became something of a spectre too.
I always said I never believed in soulmates,
at least not until the night that I met you.

The bathroom walls are covered with dry rot,
and those narrow hallways are still a squeeze.
We'd leave a fan running in that overly hot
bedroom, desperate for any hint of a breeze.

I would lie here, tangled up in your bedsheets,
listening to the Mexican place across the street
take out their trash every morning at two. But I
never slept, because that meant missing out on you.

And you fell in love anyway, despite it all,
with that little place on Houston Street.
So why is it you were never able to fall
in love like that with   me.

Lockdown Life

by Ruth Wells

March 2020....
I keep thinking; 'when all this returns to normal'
And normal is now so precious
And I hold it in my hand
With a new awe
And a hope;
Normal never had such a draw before.

April 2020; Lockdown Haiku
Lockdown hope springs in
Through my open window with
Its glimmers of life

May 2020; Mood of the moment Haiku
There is a deep grief,
Its residue marking each
Mood of the moment

September 2020...
Anxiety
ANxiety
ANXiety
ANXIety
ANXIEty
ANXIETy
ANXIETY

Starting small
Growing until its tendrils take over the forefront of my
mind
Creeping then seizing
Seeping then unceasing
Keeping me awake.

I need peace
Cool balm
Calm
A tiny flicker of a breeze on my face;
Space.

January 2021; Lockdown Haikus #2 (or maybe it's more)
This hibernation
I choose to switch off my phone
Freedom from doom-scroll.

The only mingling
Are my hopes and fears, held here
At home; divine space.

Imposter Syndrome
Haiku(s) – The struggle is real

by Ruth Wells

Proficient poser
Though her self knows the whole truth;
Tired imposter

Impossible and
Implausible, faux and fake
Mistaken again

Waiting for veneer
To peel, revealing the fraud.
I'll be found wanting.

Sow

The Burning Man
by Aoife Khan

I am the burning man
I hang from the orange tree
To free your people from their anxiety
The filth of my ashes will not touch your skin
Instead, I will be carried by the eastern wind

I am the burning man
Good sir, please
Send forth your unsullied lawmen
Injustice is my faithful companion
Unwavering in her locus

I am the burning man
The promised Zion is a' callin' me
Let there be no concealed shame
Sweet child, know your baptismal name
The old father knows no "negro

Jag Älskar Dig, Auntie

by Hanna Järvbäck

This suitcase of mine
Is far too heavy.
It overflows
With the things she left me.
And not a single thing did I want to miss.

Scattered on the bottom you will find,
Jewellery she kept close and always mixed.
Silvers and golds.
If that is not bravery,
Then I don't know what is.

Jammed in the corner are her glasses,
To help me see.
Because one day she told me,
That despite my eyes are green,
I watch and judge with blue,
And that would make it harder to start anew.

In the middle I have wrapped
The things she told me to care for, gently.
Like the left eye teardrops from her sister,
And the blood from the heartbreak of her mother.
The disorientated mind of her husband,
And the very memory of her soul.

Jag Älskar Dig, Auntie

And the suitcase is overloaded,
With all the words,
They all had to say.
Of all the advice she always gave.
To never ropa "hej" förrän du är över ån,
And always kolla till bordet,
När du sparkat med tån.

In this suitcase of mine,
I have put in her shoes,
Although in them I will never walk.
And I cried when I packed her last words,

Jag älskar dig,
And goodbye.

Keeper of Walks

by Gail Mosley

Let's just say I'll miss the long-legged stride,
single file or alongside,
me on the right for the good ear,
walking, talking, listening,
or, like as not, easy with quiet.

Stopping to breathe.
Noticing treecreeper, robin, red kite,
a familiar flower, name, forgotten, found
in the rain-speckled wildflower book.

Searching out lunchtime perches,
riverbanks, tree stumps, walls, boulders,
bird hides,
sheltered churchyard benches.

Puzzling over maps
for the path, barn, field corner,
ready to retrace steps,
down here, yes, back on track.
Owning every walk.

I am the keeper now.

My Gam Speaks in Remnants

by Elizabeth M Castillo

My Gam says my friends Ibrahim and Mehdi
ne sont pas des gens à fréquenter. Remnants of
some unfounded fear of the unknown, of the veiled
neighbour
and their mysterious prayer calls creaking out
over the quasi-silence of the pre-dawn. She slaps
my wrist when I ask her ki dir, mo Gam? Ki posizion?
Pas de créole à table! Or "Patois" as she calls it.
Ce n'est pas la langue des gens bien!
Remnants of "simpler" times, when things spoken
coloured
the world, our tiny island, in black and white. Un
langage vulgaire!
she calls it, and the words sound like vomit in her
mouth,
more than in mine. She is the reason I was never
taught;
the reason people squint and cock their head
when I order fruit in the market, or faratha in the
street.
Français, c'est mieux! Le vrai français!
Sharp-edged remnants of colonial caprice, smacking
of self-loathing. And yet, as the end creeps upon her,
it's the "vulgar" patois we speak, when she tells me
stories
of my grandfather ki ti ene zom; ene papa; ene mari; oh!

Il était tout pour moi! and those
malabar girls, who looked just like her,
but without my Gam's greatest pride- her
distinguishing feature
(besides jet-black hair, like a waist-length waterfall):
her God-given pair of the brightest, bluest eyes.

My Little Black Companion

by Marcus Jones

It was fourteen years ago in a cold town by the sea:
We met a Cocker Spaniel pup who would join our
family.
Now many wondrous years have passed; we sob, we
moan, we cry.
All our love can't save his life; It's time to say goodbye.

He made a mark on each of us, in unique diversity.
And created a special memory book; for each our own
story.
Of runs through dunes of Aberdeen, swims in the cold
North Sea
Bright red sunsets over the hills, and the heather clad
valley

Chasing butterflies through bluebell woods, bounding
past mighty oaks
Splashing through muddy puddles; slurping at
babbling brooks
He watched the children growing up; he watched
them pack and go
Looked worried when they did not return, but still
waited at the door

He staggered past the vine grove, and lay by the
walnut tree

Dropped his ball, wagged his tail to show me, where
he'd like his grave to be.
With every spade of soil I dug, a sob and another tear
But he'll lie to rest in the orchard, and always will be
near.

Infinite treasured memories; so much and yet we cry
Our hearts are heavy the day has come when
Mackenzie must die.
His spirit still surrounds me, saying it's sad but please
don't cry
I was the happiest dog alive and like all I too must die.

I feel him smell him miss him, just everywhere I go.
My little black companion, I really miss you so.
His wagging tail comforts me, sad eyes appear to say.
Don't mourn I have not left you, I'm just a thought
away.

And he still lives among us, in our garden or by the
sea.
The brightest star in a jewelled sky, that's surely
Mackenzie.
So let's not mourn his passing; let's treasure his
memory
In a place in our hearts no one can reach, through all
eternity.

I take his urn to the walnut tree; place it gently in his grave.

Put his ball and stick beside it and give him one last
wave.
A little sob escapes me; will my broken heart ever
mend?
I plant a rose to mark the spot; the label says,
Best Friend.

Winchester In My Pocket

by Manuela Vițelaru

Early 1990s in democratic Romania

Among poets, there's smoke—
a goddess with cigarettes of import
strong and fearless,
she covers my bruised mind
with a soft, white mist...
Her breath, a summer breeze,
blows my verses like ashes
down on white valleys
of Winchester lilies.

Among poets, there're pockets—
I buried my pen and creased my paper
cold and shaking,
my withered palm closes
I'm even more scared now...
Would they forget me?
Would anybody find my voice
in silver buttoned denim shirts
of washed-out blue ink?

Retractable Pencil

by Rosalyn Huxley

Blocked. Leads long lost.
Too heavy for my seven-year-old grasp.
'Made out of mess tins', you said.

The stationer puts it to his mouth
Blows hair, which might have been my mother's.
Selects the right size. Tissue-wraps a spare.

Look Dad, I've got this fixed!
Made by the prisoners
You guarded in the war.

Turquoise inlay for wisdom.
To write a weighty line that lasts
As graphite hewn from Cumbrian hills.

You swivel and click.
The new lead appears.
You shake your head.

A woman gave me this at an
Insurance conference.
She wanted me. I didn't want her.
So I gave it to you.

I'm mixing up stories.

Just One G and T

by Stewart Arnold

It's just one G and T
a gin and tonic
to please me a little
to ease me a lot

Two maybe three,
Giggling, euphoric
Tipsy? Me?
Certainly not

Four, five, feeling whimsical
Merry, musical
a la philharmonic
slightly losing the plot

another bottle,
feeling positively supersonic
and letting everyone know
I am truly iconic

Morning alarm?
screeching electronic
hangover revenge
fiendish and chronic

Just One G and T

Price to pay for fun and frolic
saliva masquerading carbolic
stomach churns awry hydraulic
pneumatic crampy invader colic

It was just one G and T
with a twist of fate
a slip of restraint
and a slice of moronic

In graveyard silence
my name to the group
lips struggle to whisper
"And I'm an Alcoholic"

From pleasure to regret
remorse to applause
role model to villain
to hero, bizarrely ironic

Kindness Defeats Evil

by Diane Floyd Smith

What is this evil that spreads
 like a blanket covering the old and weak?
We count its cost as it weaves its way
Just as a needle threading

'Stop it now!" cry our leaders
"Wash your hands. Wash your hands.
Soap and water keep it at bay...
Distance yourselves from fellow man"

 Kindness and empathy to one another
Defeats a predator lurking
Show salutary isolation to kin,
By testing we know it's working

The deadly virus we will slay
Our Stoicism will never sway.

Reap

Sometimes, a Girl

by Ginna Wilkerson

I recall the theatre from once upon a moon.
I've entered this door, sat in the seat worn gray from
blue,
watched this stage of somber midnight curtain.
A casket owns the center, a pre-emptory place for
death,
or at least a show of dying like curtain time down.

Her service begins with sparse tones of dry sorrow
and subtle discomfort from the gathered few.
Tossed around the random hall, lights low for effect...
is it funeral or misbegotten musical, which or
what? gentle port de bras rises from the casket.

A hush falls like samaras from helicopter maples.
She appears from the depths and stands erect,
portly as proper for a matriarchal corpse - not
a corpse, but alive with inappropriate hair and
crown of carpet tacks like tiny swords.

Dancing feels like magic in this place of questions.
She dances, leaving the stage for seats unknown
where I had a girlfriend, or maybe sometimes, a girl
with the scent of lavender-incensed clothes.
Did she dance away? Did she die down and out?

Our copper-crowned dancer moves closer.
I can feel her shadow dancing like a memory lost.
She's all I have now that the girl has gone - all
there is here in my theatre of shaky starts.
A horn-ed moon hangs, like Shakespeare, over all.

Undelivered.

by Nichola Rivers

Look.
The rain is cutting holes in the sky.
Cold air met warm air
Was bowled over.
Droplets curled gently around dust and smoke,
Became heavy with it.
Little water-parachutes splat above me,
They knock loudly.
I'll let them in.
I see the future; triumphant rainbows.
You had too much sun in your eyes
You chose to close them.
Sleep now then.
The sky sheds its bitterness and so do I.
It pools and flows
Out into the world flows my cold river.
Making new connections.
Concealing the grit.

Frozen Feathers

by Joseph Snowden

Geese flock down on waters still,
the last before first winter.
Their feathers dipped in mirrored glaze,
with ripples of dark water.

Some can flee and go wayward south,
others too weak, must stay.
The old and injured in autumn's wake,
hold pouches, ready to pay.

Frost trapped feathers choke the throat,
when water turns to ice.
Three-pronged knives squirm then thrash,
then mirrors turn sharp white.

Silent songs in geese who cry,
where echoes cannot pass.
Snow once soft, now hard as ice,
no pick nor beak shall slash.

The geese that stayed now sink below,
with necks that have been wrung.
Nature and her noose for bird's,
stalled records full of song.

***

Ice now melted, in summer heat,
reveals an empty sight.
For the drowned birds that sunk,
are gone! Perhaps in endless flight?

Heritage

by Emma Ormond

I have inherited your cosmic purple carrots,
hollow crown parsnips
and bleu solaise leeks.
I pull them from your garden
on the day of your funeral,
fearful that Mrs Davis down the street
will harvest them in the night
I can't let people take parts of you
even though I've said goodbye to your body.

At home my muddy haul
stains tablecloth and worktops,.
I begin to clean and cut
blackcurrant coins of carrots,
sandalwood chunks of parsnip,
oil, sea salt and under the grill
where they soften
the lump still in my throat.

I toast our last meal with red wine,
taste comfort in roots,
that have spent more time with you
than I have lately.
Imagine you laughing at the vicar's face
when I told him there would be no headstone
and planted Glaskins Perpetual Rhubarb on your grave.

An Unexpected Meeting in 2020

by Judi Moore

I heard her cough before I saw her –
that cough distinctive as a pheasant's call.
Suddenly, after the rain had stopped
and I went out, alone, into the orchard,
she was there with me among the apple trees
up to her knees in mist. Now she stepped into focus.
"You conjured me," she said, "with all your talk
of yellow flowers and sadness, and the clearing up
shower."
I had quite forgotten how I towered over her
in later years. Her widow's hump made her
into a bun of a woman, almost as round as she was
tall.
(And she was fond of a saffron bun.)

"Hello Mum," I said. "Today feels like your birthday."
"No, it's not. I'm dead not daft you know, m'dear."
"I feel it is, here in my heart. We've had
a strange year. I miss you more than ever."
"I know," she said. "I broke your brolly
in the rain today, Mum. Sorry." "You kept
that cheap old thing for nearly thirty years?
It was old when I died." "I know. But it was yours.
The one you sneaked the cuttings into
ambling round the gardens of the National Trust."
I heard her wheezy chuckle. "You and dad never had
a lot of stuff. We kept what there was to keep."
"I hope you keep me in your heart?" "Yes, always
there."

I felt her breath – the softest touch of lips –
upon my cheek, just like the goodnight kiss
I'd get when I was six.
                    And she was gone.

On the Banks of the Cann

by Peter Harding

As I sat on the banks of the Cann,
    While I watched as the river rolled by,
    While the sun was asleep in the sky,
As I saw that the hues of the torrents that ran
    Were most beauteous unto mine eyes.
I turned to the east and the dawn,
    And the sun coming over the rise,
Where the waters were flushed with the light of the
morn
    And the sun had begun to arise.

I remembered a day long ago
    When my years were as summer is green:
    The waves were a similar sheen,
And the runnels would froth and the river would flow,
    With the copses of willows atween
In the very like style of today;
    And the skies were as equally keen.
When their sun-softened splendour divided the grey
    As the light of this morrow had been.

It was here on this very same brow,
    In my halcyon seasons of yore,
    In the sorrowless seasons before
I had burnt my bare bridle and brought me to now
    That I sat on this untroubled shore.

And I watched all the wonderful while
    As the star-slivers painted the hoar
With the shine of the faintest illusory smile
    That danced on the soft shingle floor.

I should never have left from this lea,
    From this field where the river runs nigh,
    Where the morning is filled with her sigh,
Where the song of my seasons forever shall be,
    And this memory never shall die.
So I thought, where my thinking began,
    As the willows made whispered reply,
So I thought as I sat on the banks of the Cann,
    And I watched as the river rolled by.

She Blooms in Winter

by Georgia Jones

She blooms in the winter
When it's needed most
An unrepentant antithesis of somnolence
Her defiance roared in impertinent growth

She does not need the sun
She combusts inside
A white-hot tempest to forge and force essential steel
Moulds immalleable endurance that abides

She does not need the sun

Go On, Get Rich Quick

by Gill James

You could swindle your granny,
You could ask the universe to let you win the lottery,
You could work hard all your life,
 You could play the stock market,
Invest in bonds or property
You could rob a bank.
You could put your pennies under the mattress
And watch them grow into pounds,
You could have a magic purse
That always has just enough money in it,
You could sell your jewelry and your antique books,
You could open a market stall and sell goods
Fallen from the backs of lorries.
You could write a best seller
Or back a blockbuster film,
You could bet on the gee-gees
Or play the fruit machines
Or go to the casino.
You could take out a mortgage
And pay if off when you're 65
And own a little bit of England
Or rather hold it freely
Because it all belongs to the Crown anyway.
You could marry into royalty,
Find yourself a pop-star
Or a fashion icon

Or a rich tycoon.
You could ask people what they want
And supply them with what they need.
You could go to the top of your game
Be the best you can be
Be the best that there is,
The state of the art
The number one in your field
You could knock over everyone
Who gets in your way.
Or you could just be grateful each day
Mindful of what is
And rejoice in the riches you have already.

He Carries Me

by Georgia Jones

Peering across the void
Sensing stardust and heartbeat
Seeing into muscle, blood and bone
He carries me

Centring in sunshine
Taking up space in the rain
Finding give and resolution
He carries me

My best self and my worst
Seeking congruence always
Practicing integrity and truth
He carries me

Terrain and tasks ephemeral
Rhythm constant and timeless
Feeling tribal, raw and right
He carries me

Fountains in Paris

by Beth Steiner

Light fronds of sweetened stone
writhe like ribbons
as they climb the air
around their precious water.
The young and the gorgeous
dance in the pools,
shimmering in the sun like ripples.

Wishing for peace
in white wine and smouldering cigarettes,
I found my most beautiful time.
The sweetness and excitement
of whistling seventeen,
I learned,
is found in large hats on balconies.

The whole city smells yellow,
not the gold of the stars
in those drops of bounding water,
nor the musky bronze
of every church I could not pass by.

Flickering within streams of colour
your songs of summer remind me
that all we need in life
are magnificent distractions.

Dopo Lido

by Adjoa Wiredu

the first time four of us early twenties walking along
the street leading to the beach and like candy floss
light
pinky floats in the swell into my
face eyes lips
like a film cell
romance seeps in
Projecting
the second time I was with two at the festival
we were late for our showing and went to the beach
instead
later we wanted somewhere to change
I behind what looked like a makeshift kitchenette
serving room
full of shiny glass
before i could get my bikini bottoms off a guard
came in we - the two girls in my small group - stripped
in the street near the red carpet
the third time alone wanting a beach day on a
weekday i got a train a boat and another boat and
walked to find a spot
on the beach I had a swim missed out on a beach
towel sale
walked got a boat got another boat a train and got
home
the fourth time on a tiny boat with three other couples

we headed to Croatia
it was a 40th parrrrttee until the wind changed
gripping the sides
we decided on the sleep on the boat at the laguna
the breaking sky greys sicky blues and oranges into
peach
night fell to rocking
musicians in the group played
it was 24hours before we stepped
onto land and went to our lives
the floor moved we it side to side side to side
i swayed when brushing my teeth

Hyslexia

by Simon Tindale

I've always been a measured man
who marries rhythm to his rhyme
who keeps the meter if he can
who does his best to make good time

who's evidently past his prime
who's never lost his self-control
who wants to tell whoever I'm
IN LOVE AT EIGHTY-ONE YEARS OLD.

Seniors rock and seniors roll.
To hell with old age pension plans.
It's not too late to find your soul
mate. Without her, I'd be half the man.

'I Got You Babe'

by Laila Lock

*The Vinyl Administrator said in this second
pandemic*

Catch me as I pan around,
I'm lunar crazed with dead Beats' sound,
Between the trolleys in parking lots,
We meet and stand on separate spots.
Bucket draining memory holes,
I'm still recalling other souls,
Before the files are wiped.
Checkout my creds on floppy disk
My calling card, Babe, take the risk.
Though you're younger than my trainers,
Older than my laces,
Stop! Observe my catalogue of faces,
Consigned to closed accounts,
Noting as you do,
In all your crypts and gravest doubts,
Babe, I got you.
Don the mask, we'll do it together, quick, like a band
aid,
Linked up forever.
History repeats, view the screens,
The hopes of love on Haight-filled streets.

'I Got You Babe'

Hold my bloomless stems a while,
From seasons of daisychain loves and smiles.
It's all I have left, I have run
From that dream of forty years.
Of hippy hats and bleeding hearts
And not so silent tears.
And follow to another time and place,
Microfiche wrinkle of an unsaved face,
Wasting on a renamed file,
Underexposed
On a database of T cells descending,
And of wracked grief never ending,
Not downloaded at the time.
But I got him Babe.

"I want you to hold my hand,
I want you to understand."
And don't let go,
Because you know,
As do I
Darkroom developing,
I got me Babe,
And I got you.

Reggae Love

by Chijioke John Ojukwu

My heart beats Reggae
    Swaying
        Side to side,
To the perfect rhythm of
Your enchanting beauty
That draws me,
      Tenderly,
        to Zion
Where I wait patiently
      For you:
Dreaming
Of our naked dance,
        Alone
To sweet-talking drums of
    Tenderness and truth.

My soul sings Reggae,
Like a basket of songs
    And laughter
    Plucked
From an angel's bosom;
For the joy
    Of Loving you,
      My darling
Is a fountain of delight
Sweeter and more satisfying

   Than Babylon water.
My hands write reggae
Touching and
   Holding
the unseen mystery
Of your quiet strength
    And captivating muse,
    My love;
For the scarlet cords
  Of your kindness
Binds my bloated ego
  Like the tight knitted locks
    of a Rasta:
Calling me to be
  Your faithful servant
And a better writer.

The Bramblelands

by Gracie Jack

Twenty years from where we were, I stand
by the garden gate watching the younger me
swinging free feet over the wall. Small,
and as young as the summer will always be,
with you and your dungarees, soil-stained
and torn, as you swallow the last

of the corner-shop sweets and the sun rolls back
on his thread. He licks the lawn into colour and
we laugh, talking over how the shadows will fold
into the sooner dawn and how a piece of old moon
will unwind on her spool, saying, *this is the way
it is meant to be. This is the way we were born.*

Today we have been wildlings and escaped
to some place in the forest where the trees play
the light through their leaves. Their arrows cling
to your skin until your hair is a chorus of gold,
until you look at me with those eyes which say, *will
we come back here when we are old, oh when we are
old?*

With cracked hands we churn up a wheelbarrow
out of the shed and freewheel down to the stream.
I flip a pebble and watch it drown,
while you say like this, and cartwheel another.

The Brambleland

It skitters and lives, gifted, as a blackbird trills above,
calling, *one day you will laugh and one day find love.*

Then the silver thread chimes from the back door -
a woman's soft voice and the scent of knives and forks.
We part through the fence, our secret handshake:
tomorrow we will meet on our wall and be young
again.
Now, I watch from the gate as our voices spill
into our kitchens, and wonder whether you, like me,

will ever stand in the sad glamour of rain,
your eyes bright before the lights of childhood again.

The End of Summer

by Georgia Jones

Summer to me is freedom
To move, to breathe and to live
Humid air like a second skin
A comforting and complete embrace

I feel it on my back
Like the warm hand of my mother
Everything is brighter
When the sun is warm and strong

I long for endless summer
Where I will never feel cold
Forever vital, verdant and brave
Taking adventure as it comes

So, I soak it up and keep it
Do my best to revel fully
Taking joy in heat and green and blue
Holding it tight to see me through

The Other Side

by Vyv Nugent

At the start, when they first met, the way ahead was so unclear,
although his heart missed many beats, his careful head could not decide,
and so, she smiled, held his hand, and whispered softly in his ear,
'I'll see you round the second bend, and on the other side.'

In the weeks and months that drifted by, he opened his heart,
he told her all his hopes and fears, and of the love he'd been denied,
and when she saw his spirit broken, and his world so torn apart,
she said, 'I'll wait around the second bend, and on the other side.'

And so, his life became much easier with every passing day,
and every night they held each other, and in each they would confide,
and then before she fell asleep, she would hold onto him and say,
'I'll see you round the second bend, and on the other side.'

One night, beside a moonlit stream, he gazed into her smile,
and said, 'I love you more than life itself, and even more beside,'
and so, she jumped up, and she skipped away, and laughing all the while,
she cried, 'You'll find me round the second bend, and on the other side.'

Within a week he asked of her what needed to be said,
and on a sunny autumn afternoon he took her for his bride,
and just before the vows were read, she smiled and squeezed his hand,
and said, 'I'll see you round the second bend, and on the other side.'

Then on a winter's night he found a lump, not seen before,
and so, she nursed and reassured him, and she took it in her stride,
and then she got him through the worst of it, and through the open door,
there to negotiate the second bend, and find the other side.

So soon the months turned into years, the decades they ran free,
and they loved each other deeply, without end,

without divide,
and they watched each other change, and wondered how their lives
would come to be, just around the second bend, and on the other side.

And now they've reached their passing, and the way ahead is clear,
soon their lights they will have faded, and their bodies will have died, but then,
she somehow finds the strength to smile, and whisper softly in his ear...
'I'll see you round the second bend, and on the other side.'

On Earth

by Richard Helfer

Most beautiful of things I leave is sunlight;
After, is the glazing stars and the moon's face;
Then, apples and ripe cucumbers and pears.
      Praxilla (c. 450 BC)

Only a simpleton would put cucumbers and the like
on a par with the sun and the moon
      Zenobius (c. 120 AD)

Between the poet and the puritan
I have to say I'm on the poet's side –
Though even she went higher than my heart.
The Sun and Moon are grand but far; the things
I'd hate to leave are trivial and near.
Watermelon and ripe mangoes, sweet as sex,
Luscious as truth, and easier to find;
Chicago pizza – and for those who claim
It isn't really pizza, I don't care;
The gods feast on it, call it what you will;
Shade in summer days, the fading light
Over the river as the world turns blue;
Fireworks descending from the Brooklyn Bridge,
When the gold light that always fades too soon,
Became a golden waterfall and stayed and stayed;
Some songs with sudden chords that break the heart;
Body on body when my luck was good.

On Earth

In the abstract, I know that I should love
The abstract, but I never really can.
What good is light except for what it shows?

Bin Man

by Jason J Henry

I'm just a bloody bin man,
That's what they say.
I wanted to be a dancer,
I could make it pay.
I'd look good in tights.
I spend my days dancing with wheelie bins.
In secret.
Up and down the avenues,
In and out the gates.
I'm Trevor, light as a feather...
'May I have this dance?'
The lads think I'm dilly-dallying;
'He's always muckin'about,'
But it's the Foxtrot, the Quick Step, the Moonwalk, get
down, twist and shout.
I did the Argentine Tango with a recycling bin the
other day;
A blue one, on the heavy side, but she moved!
'Where's your boots?' ask the boys, as I jump off the
lorry in to a pirouette.
An awkward landing ...Damn these Cubans!
But I'm not finished yet.
I'm a hi-vis jacket bin man,
I'm a man about town,
A fashionable male socialite,
Nothing gets me down.

Fit For a Queen

by Rosie Cowan

Make you stare, don't I? Make you wonder
Blow your tiny mind asunder
Scarlet starlet, I am fierce
Battle dress, I pierce
Your tunnel vision
Burst your bubble, that's my mission
Classy, sassy, ghetto chic
She made me, she on fleek
In my sequins, she bares her soul
I fuse her broken pieces whole
That skinny kid you called fag and poof
I got her ass covered, she bulletproof

Versace, Harlem, Serengeti
I celebrate her DNA confetti
Send her gender flip to town
Bespoke gown for a new pronoun
Wearing me shows all her nerve
I cling to every curve
God didn't give her, hell no, she create her own
Now this princess fully grown

You think I conjure an illusion
No! Be under no delusion
Her inner beauty shines through me
I the shore, she the sea

I the dazzling shell, but she the pearl
I know the grit that formed the girl
Yeah, she been through some things
She coming out, she the butterfly, I her wings
Sista, we in this together, we slayin' this scene
I am fabulous, fit for my Queen.

For Poets and Friends
by Manuela Vițelaru

The night draws near—a dull, burnt smell of soy wax candle
        fills the office room like ash or *scrum*
there're very few things lasting here, those very few worth
chasing—

Even British summer daytime can't stretch long enough...
        through empty coffee cups, *kaffeesatz lessen* or *zat*
and untold words between good friends.

The poet's mind stretches beyond the laws of
metaphysics—
        clouds smoothly harmonise on cotton candy skies
at dusk
the blinking eye of lonely hearts striving to seal
        that very moment in their verses—

Sweet stum ferments from juice to wine—
        so does the poet's heart that dares to write no-
matter-what's
takes endless forms and shapes in time
        it moulds like in metamorphosis.

A reflection in the window fades away with light
        a daylight butterfly, ivory white, dies in my hands,
its wings wide open— the night itself feels suffocating.

Then, only written memories will be left to speak of
quietly loud, pensive hearts...
a peaceful place of rest, a treasure
of unspoken visions—your heart, my dear writer
friend—
A place of memory and laughter intertwined in DNA's
of red and blue tight veins, where flowing words
leave stain
of sunset palettes on old paint, and there, the sky,
for once, looks clear.

I heard the poet saying,
'I know that no one understands and never will!'
not even wives—what pains—or lovers couldn't cope
with such mad minds; always unsatisfied...
the poet thought that they had found
what they were looking for, but had they really?
A place of escapism from the longing one may feel...
perhaps they had indeed found that place that
felt...
unreal?

Still, they wrote so freely like they didn't care,
like no one even had to understand them. Why?
What for?
'What's the purpose of this writing?', I asked the
solitary silhouette
reflecting in gold dust at dusk on window glass—

I do not know it anymore...
the same thoughtful look replied, yet with the deep, eternal glance
of a youthful face, that'll be ageing
with words and light and coffee *zat, kaffeesatz lessen*
for the poets to find their inspiration once again.
Ready as the writer's pen...

Author Biographies

Yvette Appleby
Yvette is primarily a visual artist with an interest in creative writing as a complimentary avenue of expression. She has a particular passion for poetry especially spoken word She has recently been involved with flash fiction (100 - 500 words) as a discipline to which she sometimes illustrates herself.

Stewart Arnold
I love to write as a means to express a view, an idea or a plot. It is my pastime, my passion and my soulmate. I have attempted writing in a variety of styles including a full-length play (Socrates), children's stories, short stories, song lyrics and poetry.

Elizabeth M Castillo
Elizabeth M Castillo is a British-Mauritian poet, writer and language teacher who lives in Paris with her family. When not writing poetry about love, languages or motherhood, she can also be found working on her webcomic, podcast, or writing a variety of other things under a variety of pen names. She has work in or upcoming in Selcouth Station Press, Pollux Journal, Authylem Magazine, and others.

Rosie Cowan

Derry-born Rosie Cowan is a former Guardian Ireland and crime correspondent currently doing a PhD in criminal law at Queen's University Belfast. Her short story, Little Wren, was one of 10 prizewinners from 1,468 entries in the Fish international short story competition 2020 and is published in the Fish 2020 anthology. She recently completed a psychological thriller featuring a female crime reporter on a London-based national newspaper.

Georgia Cowley

Georgia Cowley is a student of children's literature and illustration, currently studying at Goldsmith's. She previously studied psychology and child development, and much of her writing is inspired by her experiences supporting children with learning and mental health difficulties. She aspires to write and illustrate picture-books for children, with a focus on providing positive messages surrounding mental wellbeing. This poem was inspired by the heart-breaking death of Caroline Flack last year.

Pixie Davies

Pixie Davies is author of The Anxious Pixie, a blog that shares stories of their life. Their creative writing stems from a blend of their dreams, imaginings and personal experience. Including exploring their sexual identity, parenting, and being a survivor of abuse. Pixie is a disabled, non-binary, pansexual. They are married, living with their husband and three young children in the British countryside. Pixie enjoys arts and crafts, table-top role-play and video games.

Penny Dedman

Penny Dedman lives in North London with her ancient cats, and has a background in television-directing, producing and scriptwriting. She has written for her own pleasure since primary school, and in the turn of the world, was enabled by that instrument of dark magic, the internet, to discover a community of creative workshops, writers, and fellow explorers. Lockdown has reunited her with her first love, poetry.

Jess Fallon-Ford

I am a twenty-one-year old writer from Kent, England with a keen interest in the human condition. Themes explored in my work therefore include grief, loss, identity, love and relationships, seperation, regret, memory, healing, trauma and mental health. My sources of inspiration come from my own unique experiences and individual growth as well as the rapidly changing nature of the world around me. I work with a wide range of techniques including metaphorical conceit and allegory, rhyme, rhythm and natural imagery.

Whitney Glover

I'm a television production student from the U.K. I've been passionate about writing since ending a story with "and it was all a dream..." was permissible, so since childhood, or since never, depending on who you ask. Metaphor, the grotesque, and explorations of the body are common themes in my poetry. I hope to have a long and creative career in the arts, filled with reading, writing, and engaging with thought-provoking narratives

Peter Harding

Peter Harding is a student and aspiring poet who lives in Swanage, Dorset. He attended Millfield School in Somerset before beginning his studies at the University of Exeter. Peter has a passion for the classics, traditional poetry, and making the most of the beautiful Dorset countryside, which provides much of the inspiration for his writing.

Richard Helfer

Mr Helfer has a PhD in Theatre and most of his work has been for the stage, though that includes verse translations from Corneille and Racine. Still, he's had poems in several US journals. He was a frequent freelance contributor to "The National Lampoon" in its good years (He's not young).

Jason J Henry (Jason Cashman)

Jason lives in a small village in the Chiltern Hills with his wife and three young children. He enjoys walking, cycling and indoor climbing. He is a Window Cleaner and dad by day and an aspiring writer and musician whenever he gets the time. He enjoys writing and reading mystery and spy stories and has a love of songwriting, poetry and anything funny.

Rosalyn Huxley

Rosalyn Huxley works for a major charity encouraging people to leave gifts in their wills. She is writing a novel about a woman who inherits a flat in a care home and has to pretend to be older than she really is in order to stay. Her poetry also focusses on the ageing process and how to deal with death. She lives in Dorset by the sea and walks a lot.

Gracie Jack (Laura Potts)

Laura Potts is a writer from West Yorkshire. A recipient of the Foyle Young Poets Award, her work has been published by Aesthetica, The Moth and The Poetry Business. Laura became one of the BBC's New Voices in 2017. She received a commendation from The Poetry Society in 2018 and was shortlisted for The Edward Thomas Fellowship, The Rebecca Swift Women Poets' Prize and The Bridport Prize in 2020'.

Gill James

Born in Helensburgh, Scotland, and raised in the north east, Gillian James was a secondary headteacher for 19 years, in two large comprehensives in the north west, where she now lives. Retired, married with a son who fled south, she has a passion for words, written and read, travel, dabbling in watercolours, and sharing stories, a grandson on each knee.
Contact email: *gh.james@icloud.com*

Georgia Jones

Georgia is a Senior Lecturer at Bournemouth University, where she specialises in predator ecology and conservation; she currently works on sharks, birds of prey and mustelids. Georgia has acquired quite the menagerie, including two dogs, a cat, two parrots, three chickens and a pony! Her husband knew what he was letting himself in for when he married her. She loves to surf, rock climb, horse ride, skateboard and she writes when the feeling takes her.

Marcus Jones

Marcus Jones was first published in a magazine when he was twelve and has recently taken early retirement to spend more time on an age old, but unexplored passion – writing. In one of his first submissions, Hammond House Publishing has shortlisted one of his poems (Please Bring

My Daddy Home), and highly commended a short story (All That Glitters . . .) for their 2021 'Survival' competitions. He has completed first drafts of two Novels and is currently working on the third. He also writes poetry and short stories for fun.

Hanna Järvbäck

Hanna Järvbäck is an international undergraduate student at the University of Brighton studying English Literature and Creative Writing. Born in Sweden, Swedish is her first language, however, since youth, found herself moved by the English language. She started writing creatively in English at the age of 15 and often includes a style of hybridity in her writing by mixing languages when discussing culture.

Dara Kavanagh (David Butler)

David Butler's novel 'City of Dis' (New Island) was shortlisted for the Irish Novel of the Year, 2015. His second short story collection, Fugitive, is to be published by Arlen House later this year. His third poetry collection, Liffey Sequence, is also to be published in 2021 by Doire Press.

Aoife Khan

Aoife Khan is an Irish-Bengali student at Bournemouth University. He started writing to make sense of the intricacies of his identity.

Human migration is his key inspiration — He is fascinated by the age-old stories that are passed around the world because of it, as well as the reasons people migrate — to run away, to start anew, or even out of pure boredom.

Kødiak

The poet known as kødiak began writing in earnest after an extended visit to Savannah GA, which is often called America's most haunted city. He writes primarily about ghosts, love, and the ghost of love. He's currently working on his debut collection, also called dancing with ghosts, alongside a career as a professional copywriter and designer. He can be reached by email on *copywritingisart@gmail.com*.

Laila Lock

Laila Lock is an autistic Anglo-Arab woman from Bournemouth. She lives with her eccentric family of: dogs, lizards, geriatric hens, marauding foxes and autistic sons plus a 'vaguely' neurotypical husband. She has a great love of the natural world and previously worked for seven years in a zoo. Prior to that she was a teacher. Her poetry entry details an informal administrator documenting from the time of the AIDS pandemic to the present Coronavirus crisis. It utilises Sonny and Cher's love anthem.

Victoria Helen Loftus

Victoria Helen Loftus is currently studying an MA in creative writing at Edge Hill University. Her work has appeared in the Black Market Re-view and Spillwords and she has written a screenplay for a Network Rail educational video in 2017. She was an intern at The Wolf Magazine, as well as writing for her university's student blog Inside Edge during the 2016/17 academic year. She is now part of the Edge Hill University Press team.

C T Mills

C. T. Mills is a poet who, after a brief dalliance with city living, decided to return to the rural north east. Much of his work is based around an obsession with obscure words and translation. He can often be found face-down in a coffee cup, trapped under one of his four cats, or at *@ctmpoet* on twitter. He hopes you enjoy reading his work as much as he enjoyed writing it.

Judi Moore

Since 1997 Judi has lived on fresh air and steam. Her life since then has been steeped in writing – her own, tutoring, beta reading and reviewing the work of others, and simply reading. She writes poetry, short and long fiction, and reviews.

Vyv Nugent

Vyv is an unpublished writer of poetry, short stories and a novel. His writing varies widely in content and style, but broadly centres on his unique perspective on his home planet, its colourful inhabitants, and their countless frailties.

He currently lives with his wife, dog and cat in a quiet coastal village in West Wales, where he especially enjoys walking the rugged Pembrokeshire cliffs, growing good things to eat, and then eating them.

Alison Nuorto

Alison is an EFL Teacher from Bournemouth. Her poetry is inspired by an eclectic mix of poets, including Carol Ann Duffy, Ben Okri, Wendy Cope and her former English Teacher, Dr Joanne Seldon. Alison's poetry has appeared in a couple of anthologies and she also won a local poetry competition, run by Yellow Buses. The brief was to write a Valentine's Day poem, to be printed on Valentine's Day cards and distributed to passengers.

Chijioke John Ojukwu

He is a published Poet and Playwright and has written and performed his poems at various venues including Ikley Literature festival, Bradford Literature festival, and the Leeds Market. Furthermore, he also won the Word in the City, Poetry Slam at the Bradford Festival in 2016 and the Short story prize for the Nigerian Health Care Project in 2018.

Emma Ormond

Emma Ormond is a poet from Cambridge, England. She holds a PhD in insect ecology and references to plants, invertebrates and animals feature heavily in her work. Her poems have appeared in three anthologies and she was a runner up in the inaugural Fenland Poet Laureate (2013) and Ealing Autumn Festival Poetry Competition (2014). Recently she has been writing with other writers remotely to produce new and challenging work.

Lyz Pfister

Lyz Pfister is a writer and translator living in Berlin. She is the editor-in-chief emeritus of SAND journal, as well as the author of the blog Eat Me. Drink Me. Her original works and translations have appeared or are forthcoming in Janus Literary Review, S T I L L, The Bastille, Counter Service, and No Man's Land, among others. She recently published her first book, Palate.

Helen Ribchester

She is a Lecturer in Occupational Therapy at BU. She has always enjoyed rhythm and rhyme, with previous attempts at poetry limited to light contributions to leaving and retirement parties. Shortly after moving the length of the country to work at BU she was diagnosed with breast cancer. She suddenly found poetry to be a cathartic outlet to articulate her feelings about her experiences through her diagnosis, treatment and recovery. This poem is from a large collection of her writing from this time.

Nichola Rivers

Nichola Rivers was born in Plymouth with her twin sister, and spent her childhood travelling Europe. She fell in love with writing many years ago, and falls back in love with it on a daily basis. She has written the libretto for a musical which performed in the West End last year. Her plays have been listed for the Papatango, Bruntwood and Verity Bargate awards. She writes poetry, and has almost completed her first novel. *nicholarivers00@gmail.com*

Charlotte Rudman

Charlotte is a part-time technician and a part-time student in the process of wrapping up her PhD on Sound in Chaucer's Dream Vision Poetry. Looking forward to 2021 she hopes that her own poetry can go from scribbled notes to public domain.

Diane Floyd Smith

Words had always been an important part of my life, as a child to both stories and rhymes . At the age of thirteen years moving on to the great writers like Thackery and Galsworthy, Shakespeare, Wordsworth and others moved my imagination. Such love of literature, combined with history, instilled my fascination for historical Fiction.

Having a large young family gave me little time to read and this later combined with business interests meant the years passed, coming then into retirement. My writing started at the late age of seventy years. I shifted to a new city.

I Joined U3A , where my writing and passion for experiencing authors and poets re- emerged. Writing gives me a joy I never expected

My chosen career path was as a qualified Speech and Language therapist, my main interest being neurology. Opera theatre and musical events are important in my life.

Joseph Snowden

After studying scriptwriting at Bournemouth University, Joseph Snowden developed an interest in the darker side of nature, looking at the life cycle of plants and animals whilst relating them to the hopes and fears of humanity. Frozen Feathers is a poem that looks at the inevitable aging process and the cruelty of being left behind.

A subject that he felt was both terrifying and beautiful.
Joech15@hotmail.co.uk.

Beth Steiner

Beth is a a doctor of theology and mythology, seaside-lover and occasional clutz, working in academic research development. She loves science fiction tv, live music, and her garden, and she exercise as much as she can except on pub night. Beth also likes to 'try to make a difference' at a fairly low busybody level. Her poetry has been published in various journals.

Jane Thomas

Jane is currently working on a pamphlet on the subject of Alzheimer's, working with her lived experience and also researchers and clinicians working in the field.

This year she has had poems published in magazines including; Stand, Envoi, The Rialto, ASH, Notes 62, Oxford Review of Books, ORbits, The Oakland Arts Review and The Oxford Magazine. In 2020 she was also commended in The Poetry Society Stanza Competition and shortlisted in the Rialto Pamphlet Competition.

She has recently been artist in residency at NAHR (Val Taleggio) and Hawkwood. She has just finished a diploma in creative writing at the University of Oxford and is an active member of

The Oxford Stanza II and Ver Poets.
She is an occasional reviewer for Sphinx.
https://www.janethomas.org/
Jane_thomas@hotmail.com
07951 044 998

Simon Tindale

Simon was born in Sunderland, wrote songs in South London and found poetry in West Yorkshire. He is currently working on a first collection and sends best wishes to everyone.

Manuela Viţelaru

Manuela is a MA Creative Writing and Publishing student at Bournemouth University. She writes poems and short fiction inspired by the world around her, by history and the arts.

Nancy Ward

Nancy Ward is a writer from Donegal in Ireland who has a background in journalism and non-fiction. She has only recently started exploring and enjoying shorter forms (poetry!) and wrote Time to Go Home in response to the experience of scattering her mother's ashes on the edge of the Donegal bay where she grew up.

Ruth Wells

Rev Ruth Wells is an ordained Priest in the Church of England, a mother, a University

Chaplain, a justice-seeker and a creative agitator. She has a short poetry collection published by 'Proost' entitled 'Formation' and is an aspiring spoken word artist. Ruth believes poetry is magic and can unearth in us things which often lay buried and uncover within people stories which resonate beyond themselves.

Ginna Wilkerson

Ginna Wilkerson has a Ph.D. in English from the University of Aberdeen. She has one poetry collection, Odd Remains, published in 2013. Currently, Ginna lives and works in Tampa, Florida (*ginnawilkerson@gmail.com*).

Adjoa Wiredu

Adjoa Wiredu is a writer and artist from London. She writes poetry, personal essays, and creative non-fiction about identity. Her work is an attempt to discuss what it means to be a second-generation, Black British-Ghanaian woman. Her debut poetry collection, On Reflection: Moments, Flight and Nothing New, offers poignant glimpses into everyday scenes and biting vignettes of the trauma of immigration and gentrification (Jacaranda, 2020).

Printed in Great Britain
by Amazon